# PRiNCE NOT-SO CHARMiNG

Prince Not-So Charming

# PRINCE NOT-SO CHARMING

# The Dork Knight

## Roy L. Hinuss

### Illustrated by Matt Hunt

{Imprint}
MAKE YOUR MARK
New York

# [Imprint]
MAKE YOUR MARK

A part of Macmillan Publishing Group, LLC
175 Fifth Avenue, New York, NY 10010

PRINCE NOT-SO CHARMING: THE DORK KNIGHT. Copyright © 2018 by
Imprint. All rights reserved. Printed in the United States of America by
LSC Communications, Harrisonburg, Virginia.

Library of Congress Control Number: 2018936700

ISBN 978-1-250-14242-9 (trade paperback) / ISBN 978-1-250-14241-2 (ebook)

Our books may be purchased in bulk for promotional, educational, or
business use. Please contact your local bookseller or the Macmillan
Corporate and Premium Sales Department at (800) 221-7945 ext. 5442 or
by e-mail at MacmillanSpecialMarkets@macmillan.com.

Book design by Ellen Duda

Illustrations by Matt Hunt

Imprint logo designed by Amanda Spielman

First edition, 2018

1  3  5  7  9  10  8  6  4  2

mackids.com

You stole this book? But that's a sin!
You've no idea the fix you're in!
You're now infected with a curse!
And nothing really could be worse.
Your nose will now be stuffed with snot.
Your head will ache. Your toes will rot.
Your butt will leak. Your eyes will sting.
Your back will break. Your ears will ring.
You'll scream and cry and whine and yell,
"Please help me to remove this spell!"
But I'm afraid your sorry state,
Will be your sad, eternal fate.
So please my friend! I beg! Take heed!
Please buy this book before you read.

*For Scott, Lauren, Kimberly, Henry,*

*and Delia, who are, I'm told,*

*members of the royal family.*

# CHAPTER 1

Prince Carlos Charles Charming peeked
through a tiny opening in the stage curtain.
The theater was too dark to see much. His
ears, however, gave him lots of information.
The air buzzed with murmurs of excitement.

Carlos knew a large and lively crowd

when he heard one. But never before had he stood before a crowd *this* large or *this* lively.

The bells on his jester hat jingle-jangled with anticipation.

*This is it,* Carlos thought. *The big time. The Village Arena! The biggest theater in Faraway*

*Kingdom! And everybody sitting out there is here to see me!*

An excited old man with brown skin and gray hair joined Carlos at the curtain's edge. This was Jack the Jester, Carlos's friend and teacher. Jack taught Carlos everything he knew about jestering.

"The show is sold out, kiddo," Jack said with a smile.

"Sold out?" Carlos's mouth dropped open. "Really?"

Jack's smile grew wider. "On the other side of this curtain is an audience of *one thousand people.*"

3

Carlos could hardly believe his ears. "One thousand people!"

Jack gave the boy a gentle pat on the shoulder. "You're a star, kiddo!"

"Wow!" Carlos said. "I *am* a star!"

But Carlos's brain also twitched with worry. *Hopefully not too big a star,* he thought.

Carlos's fingers nervously fluttered over the strings of his lute.

*Maybe I'm pushing my luck.*

Carlos had been secretly performing as a jester for months. His mom and dad, Queen Cora and King Carmine, had no idea he had a secret life. They'd be furious if they found out.

"A prince," they often said, "should be *princely*."

Jestering was *not* princely. It was about as far from princely as a person could go.

But Carlos had been careful. He usually only jestered at small events, like birthday parties or bar mitzvahs.

But a *big* show? In the *Village Arena*? With an audience of *one thousand people*? How do you keep something like *that* secret?

*I'm definitely pushing my luck,* Carlos thought.

But it was too late now.

The show must go on.

An announcer's voice boomed over

the loudspeakers: "ARE YOU READY TO LAUGH?"

The audience whooped and cheered. It was quite a noise, but the noise didn't seem to impress the announcer.

"I SAID, 'ARE YOU READY TO LAUGH?!'"

This time, the audience went wild. Roars and shouts and piercing whistles filled the theater. Carlos was knocked backward by the wall of sound. A part of him was frightened by the crowd's intensity. But another part of him—a part that was growing larger and stronger with each passing second—was walking on air.

Jack leaned toward Carlos's ear. "You, young'un, are gonna be great."

Carlos's smile stretched from ear to ear.

The announcer went on, "PREPARE YOURSELF FOR THE MIRTH-MAKING MERRIMENT OF THE FANTASTICALLY FABULOUS FUNNYMAN! THE ONE! THE ONLY! THE JESTER WHO IS BEST-ER! THE GREAT COMI-CARLOS!"

The curtains parted. The shouts of approval washed over Carlos like a waterfall. It was wonderful.

Carlos bowed to the crowd.

The cheers continued.

Carlos bowed again.

The cheers went on.

Then Carlos bowed a third time. And a fourth time. And a fifth.

He *kept* bowing, on and on and on, until the cheers were gradually replaced with a new sound: a sprinkling of giggles.

Carlos kept bowing. Twelve times. Thirteen times. Fourteen.

The giggles were replaced by chuckles. The chuckles were then replaced by a steady, growing stream of laughter.

Carlos kept bowing. Twenty bows. Twenty-one.

The laughter kept growing. Carlos milked the audience for every bit of merriment he could squeeze from them.

At last, Carlos stood up straight. The crowd was so wrapped up in the silliness of it all that they applauded wildly. They applauded as if *not* bowing was some kind of an achievement.

Carlos opened his mouth to speak, but nothing came out. He closed his mouth and bowed some more.

Big laughs.

Never before had Carlos felt so in control.

*I have them in the palm of my hand,* he thought.

Carlos couldn't remember any other moment in his life when he'd felt so perfectly happy.

His next bow was lower than the ones that came before. Much lower. He paused mid-bow, his head resting near his knees. Then, suddenly, he turned the bow into a somersault.

Carlos sprang to his feet, acknowledged

the newest wave of applause, and plucked a few notes on his lute.

"Wanna hear a song?" Carlos called out.

"YEAH!" the crowd boomed.

"Me, too," Carlos replied. "Does anyone know how to play this thing?"

More laughter.

"Anyone? Anyone? Fiiine, I'll give it a shot. Sheesh! When is someone going to start entertaining *me*?"

Carlos had been playing the lute for only a few months, but it had come to him easily. Music was now a big part of his jester routine.

He strummed a few chords and began to sing.

*I'm a prince who is also a jester.*
*And this is what I like to do.*
*When the king and the queen do not notice,*
*I sneak off to tell jokes about poo!*

The crowd cheered.

Carlos paused his strumming. "The other day I ate three cans of alphabet soup," he said. "This morning I had a vowel movement."

The laughter barely had a chance to die down before Carlos continued his song.

*So don't tell my parents I jester.*
*They'd ground me for life if they knew.*
*And I'd never get out of the castle,*
*To tell you more jokes about poo!*

Another pause in the song. "Why couldn't the toilet paper cross the sidewalk?" he asked. "Because it got stuck in a crack."

More laughter. Carlos strummed the lute once again.

*Thank you for cheering and laughing.*
*I promise your smiles will not droop.*
*And believe me, I'm just getting started.*
*I have plenty of jokes about . . .*

"Oh, poop," Carlos said.

Carlos was supposed to sing "poop" instead of say "oh, poop," but he had just noticed someone standing at the back of the Village Arena.

It was someone who looked very familiar.

He had a narrow face with tanned skin and dark, tired eyes.

And a very familiar frown.

It was Carlos's father, King Carmine.

Carlos had pushed his luck, and his luck had run out.

"Oh, poop," Carlos said again.

# CHAPTER 2

Prince Carlos Charles Charming sat on the cold, marble floor outside the king's study. He tried to listen through the closed door but couldn't make out any words. Just sounds.

But the sounds told him everything he needed to know.

Carlos could hear the low, calm murmur of King Carmine's voice. Low and calm were good signs.

But the king's murmurs were often swallowed up by the hysterical sobs of Carlos's mom, Queen Cora. Hysterical sobs were bad signs.

The longer Carlos sat, the more anxious he became.

*Will I be grounded for life?* he wondered. *Will they make me mow the eleven square miles of the royal lawn? Sweep the fourteen linear miles of the royal hallways? Polish the 38,000 pieces of royal silverware—including the 238 sardine sporks that nobody ever uses?*

*Dang,* Carlos thought, *there's a whole lot to clean in Fancy Castle.*

In that moment, Carlos wished he and his parents ruled Faraway Kingdom out of a two-bedroom condo.

Anxiety began to overwhelm him. He felt his stomach twist. He felt his toes itch. He felt his ears sweat.

Carlos needed a distraction. He searched his pockets and found what he was looking for: a deck of cards.

Carlos fanned out the deck. He directed his gaze to a nearby oil painting. It was a portrait of a bony, green-eyed woman holding a ratty dog in her lap.

"Watch carefully," Carlos instructed the bony, green-eyed woman. "You watch, too," he told the rat-dog.

He held up the fanned-out deck so his oil-painted audience could see the cards. "It's not a trick deck," he said. "Every card is unique."

Carlos plucked out the joker. "But keep your eye on this guy. This joker is *sneaky*."

He placed the joker on the top of the deck. He shuffled and reshuffled the cards until it was clear that the joker could be any-where. Carlos lifted the top card from the deck and revealed it to his audience.

It was the joker.

Carlos took the joker and shoved it into the middle of the deck. Carlos then lifted the top card.

It was the joker.

Carlos's mind began to shift away from the hysterical sobs coming from the study.

He took the joker and shoved it into his pocket. He then lifted the top card from the deck.

It was the joker.

"What, no applause?" Carlos asked the painting.

And Carlos shuffled and shuffled again.

No matter what he did to those cards, the joker always appeared on the top of the deck.

It looked like sorcery, but the trick was just a little sleight of hand. Carlos knew how to palm cards. No matter how many times he shuffled the deck, the card he wanted was always hidden in his hand, ready to be revealed whenever he felt like it.

Jack the Jester had taught Carlos the trick. Jack called it "The Sneaky Jester." Carlos didn't use The Sneaky Jester in his stage act, but he practiced it all the time. Card tricks kept his hands busy and helped to calm his nerves.

"Boo-hoo-hoo-hooooooo!" From behind the door, Queen Cora sobbed with renewed vigor, but Carlos hardly heard her anymore. His attention never strayed from the cards.

Eventually, the study door opened. King Carmine stepped into the hall. He closed the door behind him, placed his back against the wall, and slid down to take a spot on the floor beside Carlos.

The king rubbed his temples with his fingertips. The man looked like he had a headache all over.

"Your mother's a little upset," the king said finally.

"Yeah," Carlos replied.

WAAAAAAH!

"Do you understand *why* she's upset?"

"Because I'm a jester?"

"No," the king said. "Well, yes. But there's more. Your mother is *also* upset because you broke a promise to her. You broke a promise to me, too."

"I'm sorry," Carlos said right away.

The king knew a knee-jerk apology when

he heard one. He ignored it and continued, "You promised your mother and me that your jestering would be a *hobby*. You promised us that this hobby would never leave the privacy of the castle. That's why we allowed you to continue your training with Jack." The king sighed. "We trusted you. And you lied to us. You jestered outside the castle. You jestered all across the kingdom. And today you jestered in a one-thousand-seat arena. You made your mother and me look foolish in front of our royal subjects."

The words hit Carlos like a punch in the gut. It was true. He had made a fool out of his mom and dad. In his song, Carlos had mocked their ignorance. He didn't *mean* to mock them, but he *had*.

"I'm sorry," Carlos said again. This time he really meant it.

"Thank you," the king replied. "Your mother and I have discussed your actions. After much deliberation, I have decided what to do with you."

"Are you going to send me to the dungeon?" Carlos asked.

The king's eyebrows shot up. "What? Why on earth would I— We don't even *have* a dungeon!" The king gave Carlos an irritated look. "Carlos, just shush. It has not been a good day."

Carlos shushed.

The king paused a moment to organize his thoughts. "I understand why you broke your promise to your mother and me."

"You do?" Carlos asked.

The king nodded. "You need to entertain people."

"Yes!" Carlos was surprised that his father could even *begin* to understand this. "I *love* to entertain people."

"And you feel that being a prince doesn't give you any *chance* to entertain people," the king said.

"That's right!" Carlos nearly shouted.

"But that's not true, son," the king said.

"Princes have *many* opportunities to entertain people."

"They do?" Carlos searched his memory. He couldn't remember the last time he *ever* saw a prince be entertaining.

The king nodded. "Princes do entertain people. I just need to teach you how."

Carlos loved his dad. He loved his dad *a lot*. But Carlos thought King Carmine was the least entertaining person in the history of the world.

*Dad is going to teach* me *to be entertaining?* he thought. *Come on!*

The king continued, "You are a very entertaining person, Carlos. But you need to learn how to entertain people in a *princely* way."

Carlos didn't like where this conversation was going. "A princely way?"

"Yes. A princely way." The king rose to his feet. His idea seemed to invigorate him. "How would you like to entertain an audience of *ten thousand* people?"

Carlos's mouth dropped open. *Ten thousand people?!* That was ten times more than the audience at the Village Arena!

Carlos sprang up off the floor. "I'd *love* to do that! That would be amazing!"

"It's possible, son," the king said. "It's more than possible; it's *probable*."

"Probable! That means it's pretty much going to happen, right?" Carlos asked. "I'm going to entertain ten thousand people?"

"Yes," the king confirmed. "*If* you entertain them in a princely way."

There was that phrase again: *a princely way*.

Carlos slowly raised an eyebrow. "How do I entertain ten thousand people in a princely way?"

"By jousting!" the king announced.

"By jousting?" Carlos asked.

"Yes! Jousting is a noble sport where proud, princely warriors show off their skills and test their bravery." The king's normally tired eyes sparkled. "Two brave souls face each other on the field of competition. Each is on horseback. Each carries a lance."

"What's a lance?" Carlos asked.

"A big pointy stick," the king explained. "As the crowd roars with excitement, the jousters charge toward each other! Each one takes careful aim!"

"Aim?" Carlos asked. "What are they aiming?"

"They're aiming the lances!"

"The lances?" Carlos asked.

"The big pointy sticks," the king explained.

"What are they aiming the big pointy sticks *at*?" Carlos asked.

"Each other!" the king replied.

*"Each other?!"*

"Yes!" The king was practically skipping with delight. "Each jouster uses a big pointy stick to try to knock the other guy off his horse!"

"WHY?!" Carlos yelled.

"FOR FUN!" the king yelled back joyously. "And they do it before a very large audience of loyal subjects!"

The king let these words hang in the air for a long moment. Then he let out a long, happy sigh.

"So," the king said finally, "what do you think?"

"I think we should build a dungeon," Carlos replied.

# CHAPTER 3

Prince Carlos Charles Charming stomped down the twisty corridors of Fancy Castle, grumbling every step of the way.

*Jousting is entertaining? Really?* he thought. *Getting stabby on horseback is entertaining? To who? Not me!*

Carlos's stomps got a little stompier.

*I'll have to wear armor!* he thought.

Carlos's mind flashed back to the last time he was forced to wear armor.

*Ugh. Armor is so heavy. And hot. And noisy. And uncomfortable.*

*Stomp! Stomp! Stomp!*

Another thought came to Carlos. *I'll have to ride a horse!*

This was more bad news. Carlos and the royal horse, Cornelius, were not on speaking terms. Horses don't speak, of course, but if Cornelius *could* speak, Carlos would be the last person he would speak to.

If Cornelius had his way, he would beat the poop out of Carlos.

*So I have to get stabby, which I hate. While wearing armor, which I hate. While riding a horse who hates me.*

Carlos stomped down the corridor so stompishly that the soles of his feet began to ache.

Between each stomp, Carlos heard another quieter noise.

A familiar noise.

A *clickita-clickita* noise.

Carlos stomped and listened at the same time.

*STOMP! Clickita. STOMP! Clickita. STOMP! Clickita.*

CLICKITA CLICKITA

Carlos raised his foot. But instead of stomping, he kept it suspended in midair.

*Clickita.*

Carlos smiled. "I hear you, Smudge."

"Oh, poopers," a nearby voice replied. "You heard my toes on the floor, didn't you?"

"Yes," Carlos said.

"Poopers." A moment later, Smudge ga-lumphed out from behind a corner.

"Hai, CC!" Smudge said brightly.

Smudge was a dragon. In some ways, Smudge was very much like the ferocious dragons that lurked in the forests of Faraway Kingdom. He had colorful scales, rubbery wings, a long neck and tail, and sharp teeth and claws. But *unlike* ferocious dragons, Smudge wasn't ferocious. He was the size of a moose, with the personality of a pug searching for belly rubs.

Smudge also liked to knit. Most ferocious dragons didn't do that, either.

Carlos noticed Smudge was wearing pink wool booties.

"Are you cold?" Carlos asked.

"No. I knitted these booties for *sneaking*," Smudge said. "But they're not very good. I need to make them thicker. My clickity toenails poke through."

Carlos scratched Smudge under his chin.

The dragon's tail whipped back and forth in delight.

"It was a good try," Carlos said. "You'll sneak up on me next time." He continued his walk down the corridor. "I'll see you later, Smudge, okay? I gotta go."

Smudge followed. "Wait! Where are you going, CC?"

"I have a jousting lesson."

Smudge's eyes went wide. "Oh, no! No, CC. You shouldn't joust. You won't like it! You'll have to stab things. You hate stabbing!"

"I know," Carlos said.

"Or you could *get* stabbed!" Smudge went on. "And you'd hate getting stabbed. It's very unpleasant."

"I know," Carlos said.

"And you'll have to wear armor! You hate armor!"

"I know," Carlos said.

"And you'll have to ride a horse! And the royal horse hates you!"

"I know," Carlos said.

"That horse wants to beat the poopies out of you!"

Carlos stopped walking. He was growing more defeated by the second. "I know!" He leaned his back against the corridor wall and slid to the floor in despair. He put his head in his hands. "I know," he sighed.

"Then why are you jousting?" Smudge asked.

"Dad's making me."

"Poopers," Smudge replied.

There was a long, unhappy silence. Then Smudge said something else: "Nuh-uh."

Carlos looked at his dragon friend. "Nuh-uh?"

"Nuh-uh," Smudge repeated.

"What do you mean by *nuh-uh*?" Carlos asked.

"I mean NUH-UH!" Smudge said. "You're

my bestest friend! And I'm *your* bestest friend! And bestest friends don't let bestest friends get stabbed! And bestest friends don't let the horses of their bestest friends beat poopies out of bestest friends!" After a moment, Smudge added, "That's just common sense."

"So what are you saying?" Carlos asked.

Smudge stood up straight. "I'm saying that *I* am going to be your horse!"

Carlos sprang to his feet. "No, Smudge. That's too dangerous."

"But *danger* is my middle name!" the dragon boomed. "Actually, I don't have a middle name, so I can make my middle name whatever I like! So my middle name is

43

Danger! Smudge Danger . . ." Smudge trailed off. He rubbed his chin. "Hmm. I don't have a last name, either."

"Are you sure you're strong enough?" Carlos asked. "Remember, I'll be on your back. In armor. And it wasn't too long ago when . . . um . . . you know."

Smudge completed Carlos's thought. "When I was stuffed with fudge-ickles?"

"Right." Carlos nodded. "And your energy level was a little low."

"But I don't eat fudge-ickles anymore!" Smudge said proudly. "Now I am strong as . . . Well, I'm strong as a dragon!"

Carlos gave Smudge a little hug. "I don't

know, Smudge. Jousting isn't really safe. I don't want anything to happen to you."

Smudge gave Carlos a much bigger hug. "And I don't want anything to happen to yooooou! So we're gonna watch out for each other. We'll make sure nothing happens to us!"

Carlos smiled. "Okay. If anyone can make jousting fun, it's you."

"Oh, I believe in being fun-ly," Smudge replied. "Hop on my back! I'll carry you to the jousting practice field!"

Carlos did as he was told. He regretted it almost immediately. "Ow! My butt! You have spikes on your back."

CLICKITA

CLICKITA

But Smudge couldn't hear Carlos over all of the clickita-clickitas.

So Carlos braved the discomfort and hung on for dear life as Smudge happily galloped down the corridor.

# CHAPTER 4

"Don't forget to keep your lance pointed up," Gilbert the Gallant called brightly. "You are fighting men, not salamanders."

Gilbert chuckled at his little joke. Carlos didn't.

*Gilbert always tells a version of that awful joke,* Carlos thought. *And I hate that joke.*

Carlos hated a lot of things about Gilbert the Gallant. He hated that Gilbert was so tall. He hated that Gilbert was so muscular. That Gilbert's back was so straight. That his jaw was so strong. That his eyes were so confident. That his teeth were so white. That his dark, perfect skin was so flawless.

Carlos also hated that Gilbert was so brave. And smart. And strong. And popular. And patient. And supportive. And nice.

Oh, Carlos *really* hated the niceness. If Gilbert were a jerk, Carlos could justify all of his hate.

But Gilbert *was* nice, so Carlos *also* hated Gilbert for not being jerky.

Gilbert the Gallant was the prince of the neighboring kingdom, Ever-After Land. He was also known throughout the continent as a skilled jouster. He had even appeared on the cover of *Joust Beautiful* magazine.

Normally Prince Gilbert would be attending Princeton University, but he was on spring break. Instead of spending his princely vacation at Port-au-Prince or Prince Edward Island, Gilbert had happily agreed to coach Carlos on the fundamentals of jousting.

"As you can see," Gilbert said, "I set up a bale of hay on this fencepost." He patted the hay as if he knew it personally. "Your job is to race your . . . um . . . *animal* down the track and spear the hay with your lance."

Smudge raised his paw. "Ooh! Ooh! Hey, Gert! I gotta question! Pick me, Gert!"

"My name is Gilbert," Gilbert said patiently.

"Gert is better," Smudge said. "I got rid of all the bad sounds in your name. I got rid of the *ilb*. Nobody wants a name with *ilb* in it. So Gert is better than G*ilb*ert. Isn't Gert better than G*ilb*ert?"

"Do you have a question, Smudge?" Gilbert asked patiently.

"Yes! If CC misses the hay with his pointy

stick, can I help him out by setting the hay on fire?"

"No, you may not," Gilbert said patiently.

"It's no trouble," Smudge continued. "I have hot bref!"

"I know that," Gilbert said patiently. "But it's not—"

"'Cause I wanna help out," Smudge said.

"I understand that," Gilbert said patiently. "But—"

"And it's *easy* for me to help!"

"I understand," Gilbert said patiently.

"Really easy! Watch!"

Before Gilbert could respond, a *BAWOOSH* of fire shot from Smudge's mouth.

"That was very nice," Gilbert said a little less patiently.

"Want me to do it again?" Smudge asked.

"No, thank you," Gilbert said less patiently than before.

"I'm gonna do it again!"

"Smudge!" Gilbert was now out of patience. "There will be *no* fires. Setting jousters *on fire* is against the rules."

"But that's not a jouster," Smudge said. "That's a bale of hay!"

"But it's *supposed* to represent—" Gilbert cut himself off with a grunt of impatience. "Look. No fires. Got it?"

Smudge nodded. "Got it, Gert!"

Gilbert gritted his perfectly white teeth. He turned to Carlos. "Do you have any questions?"

"Yes," Carlos said. "Can we pretend I did this already?"

Gilbert's normally confident eyes were looking a little less confident and a little more angry. . . . Okay, *a lot* more angry. "Get. On. Your. Horse."

"I'm a dragon, silly!" Smudge explained. "Horses don't have hot bref."

"NOW!"

Without further comment, Carlos and Smudge did as they were told.

Smudge trotted to the end of the jousting track and waited for Gilbert's signal.

"Remember," Gilbert called. "Keep the tip of your lance up!"

That was easier said than done. Carlos found the lance hard to hold. It was long and very heavy. It took nearly all his strength to keep it from dipping into the weeds.

"Get ready!" Gilbert announced.

"I'm ready," Smudge said.

"I'm not," Carlos said.

"Get set!" Gilbert announced.

"I'm set!" Smudge said.

"I'm not!" Carlos said.

"GO!" Gilbert shouted.

"GOING!" Smudge shouted.

"NOOOOO!" Carlos shouted.

If Carlos thought he had trouble with the lance before Smudge started running, it was nearly impossible to handle it now. He clutched it with all his might as he bounced up and down on Smudge's back.

"Carlos! Keep your lance up!" Gilbert called.

But Carlos couldn't hear anything over the sound of his own screams.

"NOOOOO!" Carlos screamed.

The lance skimmed the surface of the jousting track.

"Carlos! Lift up the lance!" Gilbert shouted. "Don't let the lance dig into the ground!"

At that moment, three things happened:

1. With a solid *CHUNK*, the lance dug into the ground.

2. Carlos pole-vaulted into the air.

3. Carlos flew in a long, grace-
ful arc *over* the bale of hay
and into a muddy ditch.

In a flash, Gilbert was at his side, pulling Carlos to his muddy, wobbly feet. "Carlos! Are you all right?"

Carlos blinked the mud out of his eyes.

"What happened?" he asked. The world looked like it was at an angle.

"You were jousting," Gilbert said.

"Oh. Did I . . . Did I get the hay with the . . . um . . . pointy stick?"

"No," Gilbert replied, "but it was a good try."

"Don't worry, CC!" Smudge called. "I'll get it for you!"

And with a *BAWOOSH*, the hay bale was crackling with flames.

Gilbert rubbed his eyes as if they hurt. "Maybe we should all take a little break."

Gilbert led Carlos to the practice field's rusty bleachers and sat him down. "Keep an eye on him, okay?" Gilbert said to a blurry someone sitting nearby.

"Okeydoke," came the someone's reply. It was a girl's voice.

Gilbert hurried off to put out the flaming hay bale.

"Is that you, Pinky?" Carlos asked the blurry someone.

"Yup," Pinky replied. "Are you okay? You seem a little confused."

"I am confused. And muddy. And dizzy. And achy." Carlos squinted at her. His eyes finally came into focus.

Princess Pinky was Gilbert's younger sister. It was easy to see the family resemblance. She had the same confident eyes, white teeth, and flawless, ebony skin. But, in other ways, Pinky couldn't be more different from her brother. For one thing, she didn't like living in a castle or being a princess. If it were up to her, Pinky would spend all day every day with a sketchpad and a pencil, drawing whatever popped into her mind.

"What are you drawing?" Carlos asked.

"I'm not drawing. I'm erasing," she replied.

"What are you erasing, then?" he asked.

"I'm erasing you," Pinky said.

Carlos's eyebrows went up. "Me?"

She nodded. "I thought it would be fun to sketch you while you jousted. But it's not working."

"Because I can't joust?" Carlos asked.

"No," Pinky said. "It's not working because I can't capture the inner you. Your inner Carlos-ness. Do you know what I'm talking about?"

Carlos had no idea what she was talking about, but he nodded anyway.

"It's not just about making the drawing *look* like you," Pinky explained. "The drawing needs to show your *soul*."

"And you can't show my soul?"

"No. But I will," she said. "You're an artistic challenge. But I like challenges."

Gilbert called to Carlos from the jousting field. "Okay! The fire is out! Are you ready to give it another go?"

Carlos sighed and rose to his feet. "It's not like I have a choice," he muttered.

"You always have a choice," Pinky said, blowing away the eraser crumbs. "Even *not* choosing is a choice."

Then she looked Carlos in the eye. "Choose to be safe," she said.

# CHAPTER 5

Before taking another crack at the hay bale,
Carlos returned to Fancy Castle and allowed
himself to be squeezed into a shiny suit of
armor. Everything from his neck down to
his toes was covered in iron plate.

The armor was just as unpleasant as Carlos remembered. Actually, it was *worse* than

he remembered. In addition to the armor being heavy and noisy and hot, Carlos had an itch on his left shoulder that he was unable to scratch. His fingers couldn't get underneath the armor.

The more Carlos tried to scratch it, the more he itched.

The more he tried to forget about the itching, the more he itched.

The more he groaned in itchy agony, the itchier his agony became.

"Ah. There you are." Gilbert smiled. "You look good!"

"Please stab me," Carlos replied.

"What?"

Carlos did his best to point to the itchy spot, but the stubborn armor wasn't making it easy. "I just need you to ... My shoulder ... It's ..."

"Itching?" Gilbert nodded. "Happens to me all the time." He unsheathed his sword and slid the polished blade between Carlos's armor plate and chain mail, reaching Carlos's itch perfectly. He scratched until Carlos collapsed to the ground in relief.

"Armor is both a blessing and a curse," Gilbert said. "Feel better now?"

Carlos nodded.

"Okay then. Let's give the hay bale another go." Gilbert turned his attention to the bleachers. "Smudge! It's time for more practice."

"Okay, Gert! I was just finishing up." Smudge stuffed a few balls of yarn into his knitting bag. "Look, CC!" Smudge held up his creation. It was big, woolly, and pink. "I just knitted you a saddle!"

◆ ◆ ◆

As much as Carlos hated his new armor, it made all the difference when it came to jousting. For one thing, Carlos was heavier with it on. When Smudge galloped, Carlos didn't bounce around nearly as much.

"CC?" The dragon gasped as he raced down the track. "You got (*pant*) reeeeally heavy (*wheeze*). Are you eating too many (*puff, puff*) fudge-ickles?"

Carlos was also starting to get the hang of the lance. He was now able to keep the tip out of the weeds.

His aim still needed work, though. On the first two runs, he missed his target completely.

But Gilbert was untroubled by what he saw. He just nodded and said, "It won't be long now."

And he was right. On Carlos's next

attempt, the lance skimmed across the top of the hay bale.

"YES! Did you see that?" Carlos shouted. "I knocked some little pieces of hay off!"

"Well done!" Gilbert cheered.

"You did great, CC!" Smudge's tail whipped back and forth with delight. Then the dragon rubbed his scaly chin. "But *pieces* of hay?" Smudge wondered. "*Pieces.* Hm. Is that what individual hay things are called?"

"I don't know what individual hay things are called," Carlos admitted. "*Stalks* of hay, maybe?"

"A *haylette*?" Smudge said. "Could it be a haylette? A haylette of hay?"

"*Blades* of hay?" Carlos suggested. "Like blades of grass?"

"A *hair* of hay!" Smudge exclaimed. "Hay hair!"

"I don't think that's right," Carlos said.

"A hay *string*!" Smudge was on a roll. "That's it. A string-a-ling-a! A string-a-ling-a-ding-dong of hay-ish-ness!"

At that moment, Smudge noticed Gilbert's expression. "Hey, Gert!" Smudge called. "Why are you rubbing your eyes like they hurt? Do your eyes hurt, Gert?" Smudge pondered this phrase for a moment. "Hurt Gert. That's it! It's a *hurt-gert*. A hurt-gert of hay!"

"That is not it," Carlos said.

"Well, it *should* be it," Smudge huffed.

Gilbert's voice sounded pained. "Carlos? Could you . . . ?"

Carlos understood. "C'mon, Smudge, we have a *bale* of hay to stab. The *whole bale*. Not just a stalk or whatever."

"A hurt-gert," Smudge corrected.

◆ ◆ ◆

*THWUMP!*

The sound of the lance plunging into the hay bale was *oh-so satisfying*. As soon as Carlos stabbed it, he wanted to turn around, get a running start, and stab it again.

So he did.

*THWUMP!*

When the bale of hay got too easy, Gilbert offered up a new challenge: a pumpkin.

It took only three tries before the pumpkin was a pulpy mess. Then Carlos did the same thing to a cantaloupe. Then an apple.

*Wow, I'm really good at this,* he thought. *I have the gift of stabbiness!*

Then a new, exciting thought popped

into Carlos's mind. *And I'll be able to get stabby before a crowd of ten thousand people!*

Carlos was about to ask Gilbert for an even smaller target—a grape, perhaps—when Smudge flopped onto the ground.

"I'm too sleepy to run anymore, CC."

Carlos was disappointed, but he was careful not to show it. "Okay, my friend," he said, patting Smudge's head. "You did great. You did *better* than great!"

"Thanks, CC."

And before Carlos could climb off the pink saddle, Smudge was snoring. Wisps of orange flame flickered from the dragon's nostrils.

*A crowd of ten thousand people,* Carlos thought again.

"WOO!" came a cheer from the rusty bleachers. It was only *one* voice—not ten thousand—but it was a voice that mattered.

"You killed the heck out of that fruit!" Pinky shouted. "You killed that fruit DEAD!"

Carlos smiled. He clunked and clattered over to where she sat.

"I've been drawing you," Pinky said.

"Can I see?"

She handed over her sketchpad. Carlos was amazed by what he saw. The way Pinky could show action and movement in a still drawing was remarkable.

And it was a drawing of *him*! A bold, armor-clad blur atop a galloping dragon.

"Wow," Carlos said. "You make me look . . ."

"Like a jouster?" Pinky said.

"I was going to say *heroic*. You make me look heroic."

Pinky smiled a little, but only a little. Then she shrugged. "They're pretty good action

drawings." She took the pad back from Carlos. "But I still haven't captured the inner you."

"You haven't?"

"No," she said, "but I will."

Carlos heard another voice behind him.

"So! How's the jousting coming along?" King Carmine asked.

"Hey, Dad!" Carlos replied. "I think I'm doing pretty well."

Pinky agreed—only more so. "Carlos is kicking big booty!"

The king's eyebrows knitted together. "Big . . . *booty*?"

Pinky nodded. "The *biggest* booty."

Gilbert strode toward the small group.

"Your Highness." He bowed. "I am delighted to report that Carlos is a very quick study! He is doing excellently!"

The king smiled. "Wonderful! Well then, I guess it's time for me to keep my promise. We shall have a jousting tournament next week in the great Stabby Stadium!"

The king put his hand on Carlos's shoulder. Carlos's shoulder immediately started to itch.

"And you, son," the king said proudly, "will be the star of the show."

# CHAPTER 6

The big day soon arrived. And it was a *very* big day.

A joyous atmosphere swept from one end of Faraway Kingdom to the other. Long lines of jousting fans stretched from Stabby Stadium's entrance, down Twisting Lane, and to the center of Village Square.

It was like a giant party. Everywhere people told stories, laughed, sang, and shared picnic lunches. Roving packs of children played tag and squealed with delight.

Inside the stadium, Carlos stood on the jousting field, trembling with excitement. He stared up at the tiers of seats that towered above him on all sides.

*Ten thousand seats.*

Then he gasped as every one of those seats filled up.

"Wow," Carlos said aloud to no one. "This is going to be amazing."

Trumpets blared. An announcer bellowed,

"ALL RISE FOR KING CARMINE AND QUEEN CORA!"

Everyone stood. Every pair of eyes fell upon the only empty chairs in Stabby Stadium. Perched high above the highest bleachers was a private box that contained two golden thrones.

More trumpets sounded as the king and queen appeared through a private archway.

The crowd went crazy. They cheered and stomped and whistled and whooped.

From his position on the jousting field far below, Carlos smiled. Whenever he saw his parents together, he always thought the same thing: *Mom and Dad are so . . . different.*

King Carmine was tall and bony and serious. His face was marked with frowny wrinkles. Queen Cora, on the other hand, was short and round and merry. As she waved to the crowd, she giggled like a giddy schoolgirl.

King Carmine held up his hands to put an end to the cheering, but Cora poked him in the ribs. The king lowered his hands and allowed the cheering to go on for a little longer.

But the king didn't like being the center of attention. He held up his hands again.

When the crowd finally settled down, he boomed, "May the joust begin!"

End of speech.

But the crowd didn't need to hear any more. They cheered and stomped and whistled and whooped.

Then, to everyone's surprise, Cora put up her hands. The crowd again fell silent.

"And don't forget to root for our boy!"

she announced proudly. She pointed to the field below. "There he is! He is such a good boy! Hello, sweetie! We love you!"

The crowd laughed. It wasn't the same kind of laughter that followed a particularly funny poop joke. It was teasing laughter. A *bwah ha ha* instead of a *ha ha ha*.

Carlos's face turned red.

The king rolled his eyes and sat. He motioned for the queen to sit, too.

And then the games began.

"Fifty kingdoms sent their best jousters," Gilbert told Carlos. "You won't go on until the end of the tournament, so you can sit back and relax for a while."

That was a relief. Carlos didn't want to joust so soon after being embarrassed by his mom. He found a shady spot on the far edge of the playing field and sat.

Two men riding horses trotted onto the field. They were covered in armor from head to toe. One wore green silks over his breastplate; the other wore white. They slowly circled the field, waving to the cheering crowd.

"Clad in white," the announcer announced, "is Sir Milk Stache of Dairy Queensland!"

The crowd cheered.

"Clad in green is Lord Brock Lee Vapors of the Democratic Republic of Dictatortot!"

More cheers.

Each man took his place at opposite ends of the long dirt track that stretched across the field. A squire handed each jouster a sharpened lance. Milk Stache pointed his lance at Brock Lee Vapors. Brock Lee Vapors pointed his lance at Milk Stache.

Suddenly, Carlos realized something.

*You don't stab hay bales in a jousting match!*

Carlos had always known this, but he'd never *thought* about it until this moment.

"Oh, no," Carlos said aloud to no one in particular.

A man waved a yellow flag to mark the

start. Both horses leapt into action, barreling toward each other at top speed. Their hoofbeats made the ground tremble.

Lances were carefully aimed.

"Oh, no," Carlos muttered. He squinted his eyes shut. "Oh, no no no!"

But yes.

Next came an ugly noise that Carlos could feel more than hear. It was part *CRASH*, part *SNAP*, part *WHUMP*, and part *SQUISH*. The unsettling sound rang in Carlos's skull, tap-danced down his spine, and turned his stomach inside out.

That ugly noise was soon overpowered by an even uglier one: the frothing, thunderous, bloodthirsty *ROAR* of ten thousand joust-ing fans.

Carlos opened his eyes to see which jouster was still standing.

Neither of them. Both Milk Stache and Brock Lee Vapors were groaning on the ground.

*Oh, no,* Carlos thought.

Milk Stache and Brock Lee Vapors were dragged off the field. A new pair of jousters took their places.

"Clad in orange is Sir Lee Ness of Crabby Creek," the announcer announced. "Clad in black is Earl Lee Ryzer of Good Mornington."

Carlos's hands began to tremble. He needed to think. He needed to distract himself from what was happening. He needed to block it out.

He reached into his pocket.

Carlos flinched at another *CRASH-SNAP-WHUMP-SQUISH* sound.

He flinched even more at the terrible *ROAR* of approval that followed.

Carlos didn't look up to see the damage. He focused all his attention on the playing cards.

It was time to practice The Sneaky Jester.

He shuffled. Then he lifted the top card from the deck. It was the joker. Again, he shuffled. Again, he lifted the top card from the deck. Again, it was the joker.

"Clad in mauve is Lord O. Thedance . . ."

Again, Carlos shuffled.

"Clad in mood indigo is Duke L. Ington . . ."

Again, Carlos lifted the top card from the deck.

*CRASH-SNAP-WHUMP-SQUISH! ROAR!*

And, again, The Sneaky Jester showed himself.

"Clad in polyester..."

"Clad in ketchup stains..."

Not once did Carlos look up from his cards. He was in the zone.

What finally broke his concentration was a gentle hand upon his shoulder. Carlos looked up to find Gilbert. The prince's normally flawless forehead was creased with lines of worry.

"Carlos," Gilbert said. "We have a problem."

Carlos blinked, as if he had just awakened from a deep sleep. "A problem?"

Gilbert's forehead creases grew deeper. "A very big problem."

# CHAPTER 7

Gilbert led Carlos off the jousting field. They passed through an archway under the stands and down a long, stone hallway. Carlos could still hear the terrible action on the field, but it was only a muffled echo, as if everyone were jousting underwater.

"What is it?" Carlos asked. "What's wrong?"

Gilbert kept walking. "It's about your jousting opponent."

Carlos felt his stomach tighten. "What about him?"

They strode past a stable, where the jousting horses rested between matches. Carlos caught a glimpse of Smudge sleeping on his back. With each snore, a wisp of flame leapt from his nostrils. His horse neighbors were whinnying in alarm.

"To determine jousting opponents, all the competitors' names were put into a hat," Gilbert explained.

Gilbert and Carlos reached the end of the hallway. Two doors stood before them.

Gilbert pushed open the door on the left, and they entered.

It was a dressing room. Everywhere around them, jousters were being strapped into suits of armor.

Gilbert continued. "Out of this hat, a judge pulled two names at a time. Those two people joust each other. That's how your opponent was chosen. That's how everyone's opponent was chosen."

"Who is my opponent?" Carlos asked.

"Him." Gilbert pointed across the room. Towering head and shoulders above the other jousters was a brick wall of a man. His arms and legs were as thick as tree trunks. His head looked as if it were carved from stone. His muscles were so muscular that each muscle had its own set of muscles.

Suddenly Carlos got a little dizzy.

"His name is Sir Lance A. Lott," Gilbert said.

"He's really . . . big," Carlos observed.

Gilbert nodded. "He's too big for a horse, so he rides a rhinoceros."

Carlos felt his feet get numb.

"He also jousts with a custom-made lance. It has a diamond tip."

"Why?" Carlos asked.

"Because diamond is the hardest substance on earth. It can pierce through anything," Gilbert explained. "Like armor, for example."

"Like . . . armor . . . ?"

Gilbert nodded. "And Sir Lance A. Lott has never lost a jousting match."

"What happens to his opponents? When they lose?" Carlos asked.

"You don't hear much from them afterward," Gilbert replied. "I think because they find it very difficult to speak." After a pause, he added, "Ever again."

Sir Lance A. Lott met Carlos's eye. The burly jouster smiled, showing off a set of

moldy green teeth. "YOU THERE!" Lance A. Lott boomed. "YOU THE BOY I'M STAB- BING TODAY?"

"Um, I suppose . . ." Carlos replied.

"YOU SEEM NICE. I LIKE TO STAB NICE PEOPLE. IT MAKES EVERYTHING NICER."

"It does?" Carlos asked.

"YES. IT'S NICE."

Gilbert led Carlos back into the hallway.

"That's the very big problem," Gilbert said.

Carlos took a long, deep breath to steady his nerves.

*Take it easy,* Carlos thought. *Gilbert knows all about this jousting stuff. He'll know what to do.*

"Okay, Gilbert," Carlos said. "You know all about this jousting stuff. What do I do?"

"*Do*?" Gilbert looked a little dazed.

This was not the answer Carlos was looking for. "Yes! *Do*! What do I do to beat that monster?! What do I do?!"

"I don't know," Gilbert said.

Carlos's brain practically blew up. "You don't *know*?! What do you *mean* you don't know?!" Carlos grabbed Gilbert by the shoulders and shook him. "You *have* to know! You know *everything*! You're Mr. Perfect Prince! You're famous! You're brave! You're brilliant! You look like you were poured into that crummy suit of armor! You're the one on all the magazine covers! *And you don't know?!*"

"No." Gilbert's voice was almost a whisper. "I don't." Gilbert peered down at his armored shoes. "I'm not perfect, Carlos. Everyone *expects* me to be perfect, and I *try* to be perfect, but I'm not. I'm not even close."

Gilbert and Carlos were quiet for a long time after that.

"You are an excellent jouster, Carlos," Gilbert said finally. "*Really* excellent. I've never seen anyone get so good so quickly. But . . ."

"But that guy is going to stab me," Carlos said.

"Yes," Gilbert replied.

Carlos's eyes fell upon the second door at the end of the hall, the one on the right. It read EXIT.

"Well, you might not know what to do," Carlos said, "but I just came up with a pretty good idea."

And before Gilbert could say another word, Carlos pushed the door open and was gone.

# CHAPTER 8

Carlos stood alone in the sunshine about twenty yards to the left of Stabby Stadium's main gate.

All was still. The village was empty. Everyone was inside, cheering the violence.

*Okay. You're outside*, Carlos thought. *Now run.*

He didn't move.

*Come on!* his brain shouted. *What are you waiting for? RUN!*

But his feet didn't listen.

He *couldn't* run. Something deep inside Carlos wouldn't let him run.

He'd worked too hard to run. Gilbert had worked too hard. Smudge had worked too hard, too—and Smudge didn't work very hard at most things.

It was *wrong* to run. Carlos knew that.

But going back inside to face Sir Lance A. Lott in the jousting arena felt pretty wrong, too.

Carlos didn't know what to do, so he chose

to do nothing. He stared at the empty village and savored the silence.

"Well! Look who's here!"

The voice snapped Carlos out of his trance. "Pinky!" Carlos tried to smile, but he couldn't manage it. "What are you doing out here?"

"I couldn't stand the noise," she said.

"Me, neither," Carlos said.

"So I came outside to put the finishing touches on my drawing," Pinky said. "My drawing of *you*."

Carlos tried to smile again. He still couldn't manage it.

Pinky folded her arms. "Aren't you going to ask me if I found the inner you?"

"Hm? Oh, right," Carlos said. "Did you find the inner me?"

"Yes, I did!" Pinky exclaimed. She held up her sketchpad. "Wanna see?"

"Okay," Carlos said.

Pinky flipped to the page. "TA-DAA!"

It was a sketch of Carlos manipulating a deck of cards.

"I saw you playing cards in the stadium," she said. "And there it was! The inner you!" Pinky pointed to her drawing. "Look at your eyes. See the sparkle? That's what I was searching for."

Carlos stared at the drawing some more. "I was smiling?"

"Oh, yes," she said. "A little *Mona Lisa* smile. You always have that smile when you jester. I never saw it when you jousted, though. Even when you got good at jousting, you never sparkled."

Carlos knew this was true. Jousting excited him not because he *liked* to joust,

exactly. Jousting excited him because he liked the *idea* of jousting for an audience of *ten thousand people*.

As a jester, however, Carlos didn't need big crowds. Sure, he was happy to jester for a packed house at the Village Arena. But he was *also* happy to jester for a dozen kids at a birthday party.

Even when Carlos practiced The Sneaky Jester for an audience of *nobody*, he was happy. He got a sparkle in his eye.

Carlos smiled. "The Sneaky Jester."

"The sneaky what?" Pinky asked.

"The Sneaky Jester," Carlos repeated. "That's the name of the card trick I'm doing in your drawing. It's when I convince people the joker is going to be in one place, but it ends up..." Carlos trailed off, lost in thought. "It ends up ... somewhere else."

"You have that sparkle in your eye," Pinky said, smiling.

"I know," Carlos replied. "I have an idea."

"A jester idea?" she asked.

"Oh, yes," he said. "A very sneaky jester idea."

Without another word, Carlos threw open the door to Stabby Stadium and stepped inside.

# CHAPTER 9

Carlos was hardly through the door before Gilbert was back by his side. "Carlos, what are you doing here?" he said in a harsh whisper. "I just finished telling everyone you had the stomach flu."

"Tell them I'm better," Carlos said. "I'm jousting."

Gilbert leaned in closely. "What? Have you forgotten that Sir Lance A. Lott is eight times your size? That he's the better jouster? With a better lance? Who rides a rhinoceros? And he *reeeally* enjoys hurting people?"

"But I have a plan," Carlos said.

"You have *a plan*?" Gilbert asked. "What plan?"

"A *secret* plan," Carlos said.

"A secret plan?" Gilbert frowned. "What if your secret plan doesn't work?"

Carlos didn't answer that question. He strode down the long hall toward the horse stables.

"Smudge," Carlos called. "Time to get up. We're jousting."

Smudge rolled over. "I don't wanna go to school."

"SMUDGE!" Carlos shouted. "WE GOTTA GET READY!"

Carlos's sharp words snapped Smudge out of his slumber. A fireball of surprise leapt from the dragon's mouth and barbequed the butt of a horse in a neighboring stall. The horse let out a whinny of rage.

It was a *very familiar-sounding* whinny of rage.

The angry horse locked eyes with Carlos.

Carlos's eyes went as wide as dinner plates. "What is Cornelius doing here?"

"One of the other horses got sick, CC," Smudge explained. "So Cornelius was sent over as a substitute."

Smudge turned to Cornelius, who was

now stomping his hooves and foaming at the mouth. "Sorry I burned your bummy-bum!" Smudge said.

But Cornelius was in no mood to accept apologies—especially if the apology was from a friend of Carlos.

*No doubt about it,* Carlos thought. *Someday that horse is going to beat the poop out of me.*

Gilbert put his hand on Carlos's shoulder. "Carlos, are you *sure* you want to joust?" he asked.

"Yes," Carlos said.

Gilbert smiled. "Then you, my friend, are a brave and noble prince."

"Wow. Thank you," Carlos replied. When

a brave and noble prince like Gilbert the Gallant calls you a brave and noble prince, it *means* something.

But Carlos knew that being a brave and noble *prince* wouldn't help him survive a joust against Sir Lance A. Lott. The only way he'd survive was to be a brave and noble *jester*.

# CHAPTER 10

"IT IS TIME FOR THE MAIN EVENT!" the announcer crowed.

The final two jousters of the day rode out onto the Stabby Stadium field. Both men were covered from head to toe in suits of armor, but it was easy to tell which jouster was which. Carlos's armor was slim and narrow—a good fit for his gangly frame. Sir Lance A. Lott's armor, on the other hand, was nearly as wide as it was tall, to better accommodate his broad shoulders and rippling muscles.

"Riding the rhinoceros and clad in blood red is Sir Lance A. Lott of Carnage Caverns!"

There were some cheers from the stands, but they were drowned out by a barrage of boos.

"Riding the dragon with the pink saddle . . ." the announcer began.

Smudge smiled and waved. "Hai, everybody!" he shouted.

The announcer continued, ". . . is Prince Carlos Charles Charming of Faraway Kingdom!"

The cheers, whistles, and whoops were deafening. The Faraway Kingdom subjects had taken Queen Cora's message to heart. They would root for her boy. They would root for their prince.

King Carmine was all smiles. Queen Cora clapped with delight. She blew Carlos a kiss that looked wet and lipstick-y.

The jousters took their places at each end of the track. A squire handed Lance A. Lott his lethal, diamond-tipped lance. Another squire tucked an ordinary wooden lance into the crook of Carlos's arm. Even from the cheap seats, Carlos's weapon looked piti-ful compared to what Lance A. Lott held.

This was it. The big moment was about to begin. The local boy squaring off against an experienced warrior. An undefeated jouster. A ruthless, pitiless hulk.

The crowd fell into an eerie silence.

The man carrying the yellow flag appeared on the field.

He held the flag above his head.

The crowd held its breath.

The man lowered his arm.

The *SNAP* of the flag echoed across the stadium.

And, like flipping a switch, the silence was crushed by the crowd's roaring, shrieking,

screeching, hooting, jeering, stomping pandemonium of raw emotion.

Smudge and the rhino pounded forward.

Smudge seemed invigorated by the noise. He ran faster than he ever had before. Carlos's armor clanked and clunked and rattled like it never had before.

Carlos was unsteady in the saddle.

Standing on the sidelines, Gilbert gritted his teeth. "Come on, Carlos," he muttered.

The rhinoceros couldn't run as fast as Smudge. But what he lacked in speed, he made up for in sheer power. He was as unstoppable as an avalanche. Lance's lance was straight and steady. Its diamond tip flickered and flashed in the afternoon sun. It was aimed straight for Carlos's chest.

Carlos continued to bounce wildly. His lance weaved back and forth, pointing at nothing in particular.

Everyone in the stands seemed to sense that Carlos was in big trouble. A collective gasp swept through the crowd as the slapping of dragon paws and the thunder of rhino feet grew in intensity.

It was over in an instant.

Lance A. Lott swatted Carlos's lance to one side as if it were nothing more than a pesky mosquito. He plunged his diamond-tipped lance into Carlos. The lance had no trouble piercing Carlos's armor. It also had no trouble coming out the other side.

Carlos was run through.

Lance A. Lott raised his anvil-size fists in victory.

He was greeted not by cheers but by a stadium full of troubled murmurs.

Carlos remained on Smudge for a few terrible seconds before slumping off the pink saddle and into the dirt.

Smudge's eyes went wide. "CC?" he squeaked. "CC, are you okay?"

A horrible cry from Queen Cora echoed through the stadium. It was followed by a scattering of alarmed shouts from the crowd.

"Carlos!" Gilbert ran to where the body lay, but Smudge blocked his path.

"No, Gert! Don't touch CC! The doctor is coming!"

A bearded doctor, wearing white scrubs and carrying a black medicine bag, raced onto the field. He knelt beside the lifeless body. He put his ear against the armored chest. He felt the armored wrist for a pulse. He peeked through the armored face visor.

The doctor stood up to address the crowd. "Prince Carlos Charles Charming," he said, "is gone. *Really* gone."

The doctor pulled off Carlos's helmet.

There was no head inside. The armor was empty.

The crowd gasped in surprise and confusion.

"Ooh, jiminy!" Smudge said. The dragon was supposed to act surprised, but he couldn't quite pull it off. Instead, he started to giggle. "Oh, jiminy, jiminy, jiminy!" he said between fiery snorts of glee.

"But don't worry, Your Highness," the doctor shouted up to the king. "I can cure invisibility!"

The doctor shed his scrubs. Underneath was a lime-green outfit that jingle-jangled with every movement. He reached into his doctor's bag, pulled out a jester hat, and put it on. The doctor pulled off his beard.

Carlos stretched out his arms. "TA-DAA!"

Gilbert's mouth dropped open. "You're alive!"

"Oh, hai, CC!" Smudge giggled.

"Oh, hai, Smudge!" Carlos replied. "And that's how you do The Sneaky Jester without a deck of cards."

"I like it!" Smudge said.

The crowd liked it, too. Ten thousand jousting fans switched from expressions of horror to laughter.

The laughter was cut short by a shout from the royal box.

"Carlos!" Queen Cora was beside herself. "I thought . . . I thought . . ."

"I'm sorry, Mom. I'm sorry, Dad," Carlos called out. "But if I had jousted . . . Well, you saw what would've happened."

"It's true, Your Highnesses," Gilbert said. "I know Sir Lance A. Lott's terrible reputation all too well. If Carlos had jousted, he would have been seriously hurt. Or worse."

"HE'S GONNA GET WORSE RIGHT NOW!" Lance A. Lott boomed. He stood a few yards away. His sword was drawn.

Gilbert drew his own sword. "You won the joust, Lance. Time to walk away."

*Dang,* Carlos thought. *Gilbert might not be perfect, but he's a lot cooler than I realized.*

Lance A. Lott stepped closer. "I DIDN'T WIN THE WAY I WANTED TO! I WIN BY GETTING STABBY!"

"Not today, you don't," Gilbert said in a low steady voice.

"I'LL PROVE YOU WRONG," Lance A. Lott sneered. "TODAY, I'LL STAB YOU BOTH!"

With fire in his eyes, Lance A. Lott lunged toward them.

With fire in his eyes, Gilbert lunged toward Lance A. Lott.

With fire in his mouth, Smudge BAWOOSHED!

And that was pretty much that.

"OWIE! OWIE! OWIE!" Lance A. Lott
whimpered and whined as he ran away in a
red-hot suit of armor.

"See, Gert?" Smudge said. "I told you my
hot bref is useful!"

"Yes," Gilbert said. "I can see that."

"If you want to thank me, you may pet
my head," Smudge suggested.

Gilbert pet Smudge's head.

"Oh, that feels pleasant!" Smudge said.

"You're good at this, Gert. You must pet my head more often."

King Carmine's voice echoed down to the field below. "Son," he said, "I am so very glad you're safe. And I am sorry I put you in harm's way."

Carlos was suddenly aware of how very public this conversation was.

"You're a very clever young man, aren't you?" the king continued.

Carlos shrugged.

"No false modesty, now. You are very clever," the king said. "And, after catching your show at the Village Arena, I can verify that you are *also* very entertaining."

Carlos felt happy tingles all over. "You . . . You liked my show?" he asked.

"I liked your show, son," the king said.

Carlos smiled so wide that his face began to hurt.

The king went on, "In fact, I was hoping you'd perform a few minutes of your show right now. If you wish."

The crowd let out a wild, joyous roar of approval, but Carlos hardly heard them.

The jester prince looked up into the smiling face of his dad.

He couldn't remember a moment in his life when he'd felt so perfectly happy.

# The fourth
# Prince Not-So Charming
# book is out now!

# ABOUT THE AUTHOR

Roy L. Hinuss is the authorized biographer of the Charming Royal Family. He is also fond of the occasional fart joke. When he isn't writing about Prince Carlos Charles Charming's many adventures, he can be found in his basement laboratory, making batches of homemade Brussels sprout ice cream.